Lenny's Lost Spots

Published in the United States by
QEB Publishing, Inc.
23062 La Cadena Drive
Laguna Hills
Irvine
CA 92653

Library of Congress Control Number 2004101821

ISBN 1-59566-005-4

Written by Celia Warren
Designed by Alix Wood
Editor Hannah Ray
Illustrated by Genny Haines

Series Consultant Anne Faundez
Creative Director Louise Morley
Editorial Manager Jean Coppendale

Printed and bound in China

Lenny's Lost Spots

Celia Warren

QEB Publishing, Inc.

Lenny was a ladybug.
He was red with black spots.

In the morning, Lenny counted his spots:
One, two, three, four, five, six.

But in the afternoon, Lenny said,
"Where are my spots?
Where have they gone?
This morning I had six
but now I have none."

Lenny looked once.
Lenny looked twice.
He thought his spots
were on some dice.
But he was wrong.

Lenny looked down.
Lenny looked up.
He thought his spots
were on a pup.
But he was wrong.

11

Lenny looked high.
Lenny looked low.
He thought his spots
were on a bow.
But he was wrong.

Lenny looked here.
Lenny looked there.
He thought his spots
were on a chair.
But he was wrong.

Lenny looked near.
Lenny looked far.
He thought his spots
were on a car.
But he was wrong.

16

Lenny looked left.
Lenny looked right.
He thought his spots
were on a kite.
But he was wrong.

Lenny went out in the rain.
He said, "My spots are back again."

And he was right.

What do you think?

What color is Lenny?
What color are his spots?

Can you count the
puppy's spots?

How did Lenny lose his spots?

Can you see
the spots in
this picture?
Are they
Lenny's spots?

Parents' and teachers' notes

- After reading and discussing the story, identify the rhymes and the refrain ("But he was wrong").
- Re-read the story, encouraging your child to join in with the rhyming words and the refrain.
- Count to six on your fingers. Then count Lenny's spots in the story. Give your child a ladybug template, made from cardboard, with six legs and a red body. Provide your child with black paper spots and glue. Help your child to select six spots and to glue them in place. Count the spots, to reinforce the idea of the number six.
- Can your child remember an occasion when he/she was lost, or had lost something precious to him/her. How did he/she feel?
- Discuss who your child should safely approach if he/she is ever lost – consider different locations, e.g. in the supermarket, in your neighborhood, in a shopping mall, etc.
- Collect pairs of opposites, beginning with the directions Lenny looked in the story (e.g. "right/left," "down/up"). Which words are not opposites? (E.g. "once/twice.")
- Fill a "grab bag" with tactile objects. Let your child dip his/her hand into the bag to see what he/she can find and identify by touch.
- Ask your child to draw a poster advertising a lost valuable or pet.
- Draw attention to the alliteration in the title of the story. Think of some other names beginning with "L" that the ladybug might have had.
- Ask your child to retell the story in his/her own words.
- Look at the concepts of "wet" and "dry" using a sand tray or sandbox. Encourage your child to experiment with water to wash sand off toys. What else do we use water for? E.g. drinking, brushing our teeth, washing the dishes, bathing.
- Find out more about the insect world and real ladybugs. Where do they live? What do they eat? Do they always have the same number of spots?